PATCH

Book #3 in the TIME SOLDIERS' SERIES

Created & Photographed by
ROBERT GOULD

Illustrated and digitally mastered by
EUGENE EPSTEIN

Written by
KATHLEEN DUEY

Rob sighed. "We're ready. We've been ready for nearly a year."

"The new gear we bought is great," Mariah said. "I just wish we could use it."

Jon held up one of their new walkie-talkies.
"We're set. All we need now is the time portal."

Adam nodded. "Do you think it will ever
come back?"

4

Mikey frowned. "The first time we saw the portal was on a Saturday morning, remember?"

"After a rain," Mariah said quietly.

Adam nodded. "It poured last night."

Mikey glanced at Rob. "Let's gear up."

"I just know it'll be there this time," Mikey said to Bernardo.

Everyone was excited, walking fast down the path to the woods.

At the same time, in a sophisticated mobile laboratory, two men in dark suits stared at a 3-D holographic screen. One of them smiled.

"This is it! The temporal continuum is distorting. How's the signal from the 3XVP device?"

His partner keyed the receiver. "Perfect. I installed it in their camera myself."
The man looked back at the screen. "The temp-distort measurements are higher than usual."

time portal control

zone 1

01 2344 2587 7844 1233 2898588 A3847
212431 c685 7657 322443 4543 35365 34
244453 0050858 666353 2223 435 7768

zone 2

Back in the woods, the Time Soldiers could not believe their eyes.

"It's here!" Mariah whispered.

Rob swallowed hard, scared and excited.

They walked forward together.

"I hear the ocean," Mikey said.
Adam glanced at him. "Me, too."
They walked faster through the swirling light.
A second later they were standing in deep
white sand.

Rob stared. The beach was deserted. It was amazingly clean, like the dinosaurs' homeland had been—not a single piece of trash anywhere

Mariah turned. "Hear that? Someone's crying."
Adam stood beside her. "Over there. It's coming
from that cave."
They walked closer.

"Someone's in big trouble," Jon said quietly.
Rob strained to hear better. "It's a kid."
Mikey stood up. "Then we have to help."

0:12(X200%)

"Wait!" Rob said. But it was too late.
Mikey was already racing toward the opening
in the rock.

Rob chased his brother. "Hold on, Mikey!" he pleaded. "You don't know what's in there!"

Mikey whirled around to look at him. "Listen!" The crying was louder this close to the cave. The kid sounded scared to death.

Rob glanced back. The others were coming fast. He let go of Mikey's shoulders and followed him into the cave.

The men in dark suits continued to study the detailed images in the holograph.

"These Originals are good material," one said. "Certainly brave enough."

The other man just nodded and checked the band density on the receiver. The images were perfect. They were going to see a lot of this. He smiled. It was almost like being there.

"My head hurts," Jon said, "really bad."

Rob frowned. "You OK?"

"Look!" Mikey whispered hoarsely before Jon could answer.

Rob turned and stared. What was going on here?

"Are you all right?" he asked. "We heard you crying and—"

"I never cry, you dullard," the prisoner growled.

Mikey flipped on his flashlight. "We'll help you."
"Then get that strange torchlight away from
me and get on with it."
It was a girl, he realized. "Who are you?"

"Name's Julia. Now cut me loose, ye sluggards. Calico Jack is usin' me and my father as bait— he wants a battle with The Sapphire."
Mikey pulled out a pocket tool and cut the ropes. "Pirates?" Mariah whispered. Rob nodded.

"Look at this!" Adam breathed.
Rob turned. He stared, then walked closer.
"Is that gold? Are those jewels real?"
He sifted the coins between his fingers.

Julia scowled at all of them. "Of course it's gold, ye scurvy-brains. Yer all quite strange, ye know that?"
Rob glanced at her, then looked down at the glittering treasure.

"Pirates?" Bernardo whispered. Mikey looked like he was in shock. Bernardo couldn't believe it either. They'd seen a pirate as the portal closed last time. But that had been more than a year ago.

Adam crossed the cavern. "What's in there?"
"Keep out!" Julia said, whirling around. "Who
are ye? I've never laid eyes on hats like yers.
Never seen shirt-cloth so strangely dyed."

Jon stood back and turned on the video cam.
"What's that?" Julia asked sharply.
Adam reached past her and pushed on the door.
It creaked open.

Mikey saw sacks of potatoes and coils of rope. "What are those?" He pointed at a box of slender metal rods.

"Boarding spikes," Julia said. "We pound 'em into a ship's hull. Now snuff out yer little torches

or Calico Jack'll see."

"Hey!" Mikey said suddenly. "What was that?"

Julia shook her head. "Don't you know cannon fire when you hear it?"

"Cannon fire?" Bernardo repeated.

A distant cannon boomed again.

"Aye!" Julia pulled Mikey to a door in the cave wall. "That's The Sapphire, my father's galleon. His men are coming to rescue us."

Mariah pointed. "Is that rowboat coming here?"
"Ahhhh, Julia hissed. "It must be Calico Jack,
the rat-hearted, greed-bent blackguard."

She clenched her fists. "Nor will he come alone. He'll have some of his scurvey men with him."

Rob stood still, unable to move. He looked at Jon, then at his brother and Adam.

They looked stunned—like they couldn't believe what they were seeing.

Pirates! No doubt about it. They were dragging the boat out of the water, heading for the cave.

"What should we do?" Adam whispered.
Mikey leaned forward, looking down toward
the beach. Rob knew what he was thinking.

It'd be smart to get away from the cave.
But the pirates would spot them trying
to escape.

"Don't gawp!" Julia hissed. "Hide!"
They all scrambled back inside.
"The storeroom!" Jon said, just loud enough
for everyone to hear.

Rob and Jon ran and hid among some barrels.
Mariah ducked down behind a sea chest.
Mikey and Adam hid in the shadows.
Bernardo crouched close to the wall.

Bernardo felt a hand on his shoulder. He glanced up, expecting to see Mikey or Rob. But it wasn't a friend.

He screamed.

The pirates came running, their feet pounding on the cave floor. "Girl-brat!" one of them shouted. "Hold fast or we'll make ye sorry."

Mikey stood up. "Hey! Leave her alone!"
Heavy boots scraped the rock.
"Over here!" Rob scrambled to his feet.
So did Bernardo, then Mariah.

"Aaaarrg!" the pirate shouted. "More brats!"
Jon pressed against the barrel, keeping low.
His headache was worse. It was hard to think
clearly. If the others were captured, they would
need him.

"What manner of brat are ye?" a pirate rasped, yanking Rob up with one hand.

Rob flinched as the pirate rapped the top of his helmet.

"Hard as Spaniards' steel," the man snarled.
"Where do ye come from?" No one answered.
Rob glared at the pirate. This was Calico Jack.
It had to be.

Cannons boomed again. They sounded closer. Adam looked scared. So did Mariah and Mikey. Bernardo was walking stiff-kneed as Calico Jack herded them all into the boat.

Rob glanced back. At least Jon had escaped.
He would save them.
A weird light caught Rob's attention.
Calico Jack was wearing a strange jewel.
It looked like it was glowing...but how?

The black water seemed endless. Calico Jack glared at them, his eyes angry and cruel.

The pirates on the ship let down a rope ladder.

Rob was wet, cold...and tired.

"Step lively, or you'll walk the plank," Calico Jack threatened.

Once the boat was out of sight, Jon climbed down the rocks and sprinted across the beach.

He unpacked his raft. The self-inflation air pump was fast. It took less than a minute.

The prisoners' hold smelled like a sewer.
A one-eyed pirate was tied up, slumped
to one side, asleep.
  "Wake up, Patch," Calico Jack roared.
  "We've brought yer daughter."

Mikey bit his lip as the pirates tied him up.
The ropes hurt.

One of the pirates tugged at Rob's gear belt.
"Ye can pick their pockets later," Calico
Jack growled. "We've a fight to win first."

Cannon shots rumbled overhead. Rob felt the deck shudder.

"I can reach my pocket tool," Mariah whispered.

"Father!" Julia called.

"Julia-girl?" came a drowsy voice.

"Those are The Sapphire's cannons," Julia told him.
A flashlight went on. "I'm untied," Mariah announced.
Soon, five flashlights lit the chamber.
Patch gasped. "What strange spawn are ye?"

They tiptoed up creaking ladders to the deck.
"Why are the lanterns out?" Rob whispered.
"My men can't take aim at darkness," Patch
answered.
"Calico Jack is smart," Mariah said.

Patch nodded. "He is that—and a black-hearted liar."
"I have an idea," Rob said quietly, "but it'll only
work if we can contact Jon." He explained the plan.
Then he pulled the walkie-talkie out of his pocket.

ZONE #2

TIME

123474
778869
020028
353 89C
-87871
77878Y

MAGNIFICATION X1000

123474356456 54547_77E6E-897767788E9
0200289W9292 344435353 8900-9U5-8YC
—8787872-988 0—0W9Q89W77878YY

123474356456 54547_77E6E-89776778
W8W799W
0200289W8292 344436353 890
9U5-8YDB7WEYW766WW
787873.966 0—0W9969.W7787

The images had become dim and moonlit.
"Do you think they'll make it?" the man asked.
The other one shrugged. "I think so. They're
the Originals...no training at all and look
how far they've come."

The first man raised a hand. "Listen."
The sound of cannons rumbled from the image.
He pointed at the holograph.
The boy's radio crackled to life.

The handset beeped, locking on the strongest signa on? Where are you?" Rob whispered.
From the far side of Calico Jack's ship came the answer. Rob explained his plan. "I'll be waiting," Jon said, "Be careful."

Rob opened his pack and pulled the raft out.
Air hissed through the valve, inflating it.
    Could the pirates hear it? Probably. They'd
need to hurry.
    "Now!" Rob said.

Five flashlights blazed across the water.
"Light yer cannons, men," Patch shouted.
"Aim at the lights! Then take the ship!"
The Sapphire's cannons exploded. The Time
Soldiers ran for the other side of the ship.

"Fire on the fo'castle!" came a wailing shout.
"The hull!" someone screamed. "She's taking water!"
"They're boarding!" came a shout.
The sound of clanking swords filled the night air.

The noise was incredible. Fire was everywhere. Rob led the way past the fighting pirates to the dark side of the ship.

"Jon?" Rob shouted. "Jon?"

" Here!" The answer came from the water below. Rob lowered his raft and helped the others down. "Go with them, Julia," Patch ordered, drawing his sword. "Wait at the cave." Quickly, he turned back to the battle.

"Brats! Hold!" A deep voice challenged from above.
Jon helped Julia into the raft.
Mariah pulled Mikey in.
As they rowed away, Rob saw Calico Jack
shaking his fist.

"The Sapphire looks like she's captured the dullards' ship," Julia yelled. "But if I know Calico Jack, he'll be comin' after us for revenge!"

The noise of the battle slowly faded. The beach felt almost safe.

"Pack the rafts," Rob said, "and meet me and Jon at the cave." He paused. There was a dark shape on the water. Was it a boat?

"Calico Jack!" Julia hissed. "He's left his ship and his men to their fates, the hard-hearted coward."

"I have an idea," Jon said. "Mikey, come with us."

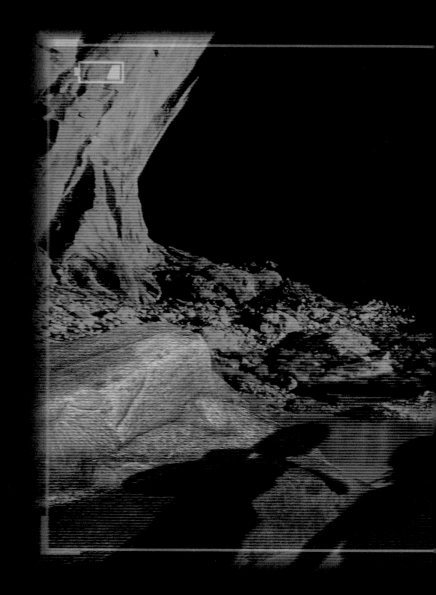

Adam was on the beach videotaping.

"Is the portal here?" Mariah asked as she and the others caught up.

Adam shook his head. "Not yet. I barely got anything on tape. If we want to prove this..."

1:59(X100%)
•REC

"Avast!" Julia interrupted. "Stop yer jawin' and prepare to defend yerselves."

Rob looked back at the water. The boat was getting closer.

"Check this out, Rob...a cannon."
Rob turned to look at Julia. "Is there powder?"
She pointed to the barrels. "Yes...but no
cannonballs. We'll need something else to fire."
Bernardo grinned. "How about these potatoes?"

Julia smiled. "Do ye carry flint strikers?"
"We have camping matches," Mikey said.
Adam ran into the cave. "The boat's coming!
Hurry!"

The men were still staring at the image.
One was frowning. "Did you see that green jewel?"
The other man nodded. "It looked like a—"

"What else could it be?" his partner interrupted. Then he stood up. "Let's go. I want to be there when the portal opens."

Julia showed Mariah and Adam how to load the cannon. The potatoes fit perfectly. Jon explained his idea to Rob. "It'll mean wrecking this..." He held up the walkie-talkie. "But it could save us."

Rob took a roll of duct tape out of his pack.
"I think it might work," he said.
"It better," Mikey mumbled.
"Let's do it then," Jon said.

Jon spotted some iron rings set in the rock.
He pointed. "We'll hang it there."
 He took the cover off the walkie-talkie
and turned the volume all the way up.

Then they raised the skeleton carefully.
The bones rattled.
"Perfect," Rob said.

"Here they come!" Julia shouted.
"Load up!" Adam shouted.
Rob prepared to light the cannon fuse.

"Ye've no way to fight. Surrender, ye little varmints!"
Calico Jack's voice echoed off the cave walls.
   Jon clicked on his walkie-talkie. "Cover your ears,"
he whispered.

"Aahhhhhhoooooooohhhh," Jon wailed in a high, ghostlike voice. "One more step and ye'll share a terrible fate. Oooooooeeeeeaaahhh!"

An instant later, the cannon fired and potatoes exploded out of the barrel.

The pirates howled and cursed, scattering as they ran out of the cave.
Their angry shouts quickly faded into the distance.

The cave was full of smoke.
Mikey rubbed his eyes and coughed.
"Can you see any of them?" Rob asked.
"No," Jon said. "I think it worked!"

He picked up the video cam and aimed at the cave entrance.

"Huzzah! You scared 'em off," Julia said.

"Hey! Look...the portal!" Mariah shouted. John focused in on the swirling light.

Patch appeared out of the smoke and stood in front of the portal. "Father!" Julia cried.

"Julia-girl?" Patch called back. "Are ye safe?"

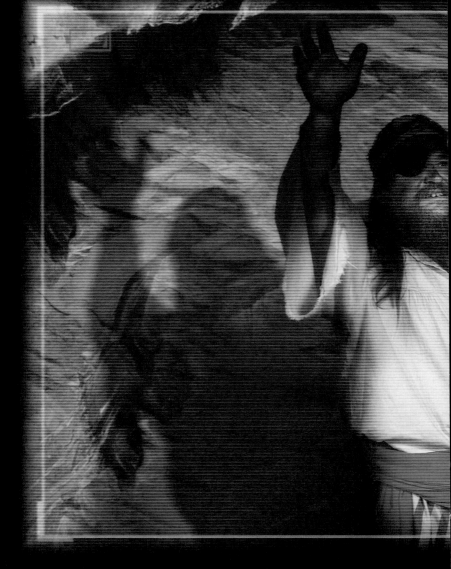

Julia ran toward her father. Mikey nudged Jon.
"Get them on tape."
Jon lifted the camera. His headache was
getting worse again. The pain was awful.

"What's that strange tunnel o' light yer wal
into?" Julia asked.

"It's...our way home," Rob told her.

"They saved my life," Julia told her father.

"I'd share gold with anyone who helped my Julia," Patch said.

Rob glanced at the others, then back at Patch.

The portal would close if they didn't hurry.
Mariah motioned to Rob. "We have to go now."
"We were glad to help," Rob said.
They lifted their hands in farewell.
"Keep her safe," Mikey called to Patch. "Goodbye!"

It was so good to be back in the clubhouse, and to feel safe again.

"Is the camera broken?" Mikey asked.

"It worked yesterday," Rob said. "But nothing we shot is here."

"I wish we could prove this stuff," Mikey mumbled.
Jon closed his eyes. The headache was still there.
Mariah looked worried. "Jon, are you OK?"
He nodded. "But I don't think I can go through
the portal again..."

To be continued...

TIME SOLDIERS®
Book # 3 PATCH

Text © 2005 Kathleen Duey
Photography © 2005 Robert Gould
Illustrations © 2005 Eugene Epstein

ISBN: 1-929945-76-0

www.bigguybooks.com

Published by BiG GUY BOOKS, Inc.
6359 Paseo Del Lago • Ste B
Carlsbad, CA 92011 USA

Printed in China

Check out all the NEW STUFF at www.bigguybooks.com